The Horse Jar

BY **Linda Benson**

ILLUSTRATED BY **Susan Spellman**

For all kids everywhere who dream of horses

For information contact:
MONDO Publishing
980 Avenue of the Americas
New York, NY 10018
Visit our website at www.mondopub.com

Printed in the United States of America

09 10 11 12 13   9 8 7 6 5 4 3 2 1
ISBN 978-1-60201-948-5

Designed by E. Friedman

Contents

Chapter One

Annie pedaled hard, racing to get home. The newspaper was delivered around three o'clock, just when she got out of school. She snatched it out of the box, tucked it under her arm, and sprinted upstairs. She opened the paper wide. She bypassed the headlines. She wasn't interested in the comics. Instead, Annie went straight for the classified ads. Her eyes darted immediately to the section marked *Horses for Sale.*

With the quick gaze of a robin searching for the first worm, Annie's brown eyes scanned the ads, looking for anything new:

REGISTERED QUARTER HORSE GELDING
Show prospect. Very flashy. Professionally trained.
$3,500. Call 795-3245.

No, she thought, *can't afford that one.*

PAINT BROODMARE
Sired by Color Spot. In foal to World Champion.
$2,500. Call 376-7991.

Annie thought it would be wonderful to raise a baby

horse, but she didn't have the money to buy a world champion or even a future world champion. Besides, that was a bit much for a first horse, wasn't it?

All Annie Mitchell really dreamed about was a horse of her own—to feed and brush, to ride through the hills behind her house, to talk to, and to be her friend. Wasn't that what horses were for?

At the end of the column, Annie spotted a new ad, one that wasn't in the newspaper the day before. It said:

BAY GELDING
15 years old. Excellent trail horse. Gentle and sound.
Only $800.
Call evenings, 444-5927.

"Call evenings?" *What did that mean? Was it five o'clock? Six o'clock?*

"Mom," she called. Annie carried the paper through the house, looking for her mother. Shoving open the back screen door, she spotted her in the garden. Sleeves rolled up and a pair of pruning shears in her hands, her mom was covered with twigs and small leaves, attacking the ivy that circled up a massive oak tree. "Mom," Annie asked, "what time does evening start?"

"Why? What's going on this evening?" Mrs. Mitchell pushed her brown hair back out of her face. She looked hot and sweaty.

Annie wondered why her mom was so mean to the ivy, chopping it down as soon as new shoots started winding their way up out of the ground. Annie liked the way the ivy curled around the trunk of the old tree, twining its way to the top.

"Pesky stuff." Her mother made a face as she gave the

vine another vigorous whack. "It'll kill this tree if I don't keep it cut back."

Annie didn't see how ivy could kill such an enormous tree, but she kept that thought to herself.

"What was it you needed, honey?" asked her mother, clicking the shears impatiently.

"Uh . . . nothing, really." Annie wanted to tell her mother about the new ad in the classified section—about the horse that sounded *absolutely perfect.* But Mom was absorbed in her project to wipe out every last bit of ivy from the world.

Dad would be home from his job as a middle school teacher soon, but Annie couldn't even mention the word *horse* to him. He came unglued and started talking about money whenever she brought it up.

So Annie retreated to her room. Lying on her bed, rereading every ad in the horse column until she had them memorized, she stared at the horse jar on her dresser and let her mind wander.

Chapter Two

The horse jar was really an old ornate tin jar that her mom had purchased at a garage sale. "Ohh, totally cool!" Annie said, when she first saw it. It was covered with fading art nouveau designs from the 1920s, but the top still fit snugly, making it a great place to stash things. Money, for instance.

Annie had been saving her money for a long time. At first, only her allowance would go into the horse jar. Then money from odd jobs she would ask to do around the house. On birthdays and Christmas, she might get a check from Grandma. Annie never spent that money. Every penny, every dime, every dollar went into the horse jar. Annie was a girl who knew what she wanted, and she wanted a horse. Now Annie took down one of the books from her shelf—the one explaining colors of horses. "Bay," she read. "Red brown with a black mane and tail, often with black legs below the knee." She imagined rubbing a body brush over a silky red coat, slipping a leg over a broad back, and cantering across a meadow into . . .

The sound of the phone brought Annie out of her daydream. Racing downstairs, she grabbed it on the second ring. It was Chelsi.

"Hi, wanna go for a bike ride? I thought we could go down along the river, and maybe stop at Cedar Grove Stables and pet the horses."

"Okay, sure," said Annie. "I have to check with my mom first, and then I'll meet you at the corner in about five minutes."

Chelsi Fidori was Annie's best friend in the whole world and the only one that really knew her true heart's desire. Chelsi also knew how many phone calls Annie made about horses. She knew, for instance, that Annie responded to every single newspaper advertisement about horses that sounded promising.

"Hello," Annie would say, "I'm calling about the horse you have for sale."

"Yes. What would you like to know?"

"Well, what does it look like?"

"Oh, it's a gorgeous animal."

Annie tried to ask the right questions. "Is it good for kids to ride? Is it well trained?"

"This horse is gentle as a kitten," they would sometimes answer. Or, "No, this horse needs an experienced rider." Occasionally she would hear, "Well, he's still a little green."

Sometimes Chelsi listened in on these conversations. "*Green?*" she giggled. "Is that the color of the horse?"

"No, silly. It means that it's not very well trained yet."

"Well, maybe you shouldn't get one like that."

"But I could train it myself," Annie boasted.

"Maybe you could," said Chelsi. "Do you know *how*? But if it was already trained, then you could take me riding with you. Wouldn't that be great?"

Chelsi never laughed at her phone calls or told her she

was weird. At school, Annie had a reputation for being horse crazy. Some of the boys in her class teased her, especially Justin. But Chelsi was a true friend. "Follow your dreams!" she always said to Annie.

At the corner Annie spotted Chelsi, long curls floating out behind her, pedaling down the river road. For the moment there were no cars, and they wove their bikes in and out of the dotted line in the middle of the road. It was a game they played, pretending they were riding quarter horses, cutting back and forth quickly to keep the steer separated from the rest of the herd.

About a half mile from home and close to the stables, Annie heard a noise behind her—a scrabbling on the pavement. She glanced back and saw a little dog racing towards them—tongue lolling out of his mouth, and short legs pumping as hard as they could. He seemed to be gathering speed and momentum as he ran. "Chelsi, wait up!" Annie hollered. "It's Spunky."

Chelsi braked hard and swiveled on her seat. "Oh, great!" she groaned. "Now I'll have to take him back home."

Chapter Three

Spunky had short little legs, a long body, and coarse gray hair. He looked like a mutt—a cross between an Irish wolfhound and a wiener dog. But Chelsi insisted that he was AKC registered.

"What does that mean?" Annie once asked.

"It means he's registered with the American Kennel Club," said Chelsi. "He has a certificate."

"But what *kind* of dog is he?"

"A purebred wire-haired dachshund." Chelsi put her hands on her hips, puffing up with pride. "His real name is Friarsburg's Frederick Ferdinand of Farnworth."

"If you say so. But Spunky suits him better."

Chelsi put Spunky in the basket on the front of her bike. "He must have dug under the fence again. He can't just run out into the street like that."

Even though the road that ran by the river was often deserted, every now and then a log truck would come barreling out of nowhere, hurrying to the mill. Tourists gazing at the river usually drove pretty slowly. But people going into town or coming home from work often sped along so fast that the girls could feel the wind whoosh by on their legs as they tried to keep their bikes on the far shoulder of the road. Chelsi and Annie had just been fooling around on their bikes in the middle of the road, but now the thought of Spunky being hit by a car made them sober up and take notice.

"Dad said he's going to run an electric wire along the bottom of the fence so he doesn't dig out anymore," said Chelsi.

Annie winced. "Electric? Isn't that mean?"

"Not if it saves his life. It'll just give him a little shock— it's not really painful. Spunky just wants to be with us, I guess."

"Hey, Spunk-dog. You shouldn't be out on this road." Annie ruffled the soft hair around the dog's neck. "You could get hurt." Spunky licked her face in response, and Annie giggled.

Chelsi pedaled home slowly, balancing Spunky with one hand and steering with the other. The little dog leaned forward, breathing in all the exciting smells.

"Spunky's about the best dog in the whole world, Chels," said Annie. "Sometimes I feel like he's almost my dog, too. Especially since we can't have one."

"Yeah, why don't you guys have a dog?" asked Chelsi.

"My brother, remember? He has *allergies*."

Annie tried not to show it, but she was disappointed that they hadn't made it to Cedar Grove Stables. For her birthday last year, Mom and Dad had given her riding lessons, and every Saturday for six whole weeks she got to hang out at the stables—watching, learning, and just smelling horses, as well as getting the basics of riding down pat. She had learned how to bring a horse in from the pasture, to brush one and clean its hooves, and even how to hoist the saddle onto the horse's back and cinch it up tight. Annie never missed a reason to go by the stables, but getting Spunky home was more important. Besides, she was still thinking about the new ad under *Horses for Sale*.

Sure enough, as they pushed their bikes around the corner of Chelsi's house, they discovered fresh dirt where Spunky had dug under the fence.

"Come on," said Chelsi, grasping the mischievous pooch in her arms. "Up to my room where you'll definitely be safe."

Annie followed them up the stairs. "What time is it?" she said.

"It's a little after five, I think."

"Do you have today's paper?" Spunky jumped up on the bed beside Annie, shoving his head under her hand, begging for attention.

"I think so. My mom probably left it right by Dad's chair. She's being extra nice to him 'cause he's so worried."

"About what?"

"He's afraid he'll get laid off at the mill," said Chelsi.

"What does that mean?" asked Annie.

"It means he won't have a job. I hear them talking about it at night, when they think I'm asleep. About money and being able to afford stuff."

"Oh," said Annie, unsure of what else to say. She stroked Spunky, whose head lay on her knee. "Do you think it's evening yet?"

"Yeah, I think it's evening," said Chelsi. "'Cause that's when my dad gets home from work. Why?"

"Because there's a horse that sounds *absolutely perfect* in today's classified ads. Sorry, Spunk-dog," she said, rearranging him on the bed. "Come on, let's go find the paper."

Chelsi rolled her eyes. "*Absolutely perfect*? Do you know how many times you've said that?"

Shuffling through the sports section, the grocery ads,

and the community news, Annie finally found the classified ads. She thought she had the telephone number memorized, but checked to make sure. Her hands trembled as she punched in the numbers.

Rocking backward on a kitchen stool, Chelsi peered at the section and began to read. "What's an aqua gelding?"

"Not aqua," answered Annie. "A-Q-H-A. It's initials for American Quarter Horse Association. It means the horse is registered. It's a purebred. It has a certificate—like Spunky." But her mind was on the gentle bay gelding advertised for $800. "Shh. It's ringing . . . Yes ma'am. This is Annie Mitchell. I'm calling about your horse for sale." Annie tried to make her voice sound grown-up, but her heart raced with anticipation. "Is it still available?" she asked in a squeaky voice.

"Well, for now he is," answered a woman with a Western drawl. "We've had a lot of calls on him already. Is he for you? How old are you?"

Annie listened patiently to the woman's description. The horse was a teenager, she told her, just the right age for a first horse. The woman said that young horses are not usually good choices for a first horse because they don't have much sense yet. "Older horses are a good bet 'cause they've been around the barn once or twice."

This sounded like the right horse—her very own first horse! "Let me talk to my parents," she said. "Maybe we can make an appointment to come out and see him. What's his name?"

"We call him Red," said the woman. "Nothing fancy—he's just a nice plain old bay horse."

Red. Red. Annie rolled it over and over in her mind a couple of times before snapping back to reality. She glanced over at Chelsi, who was watching intently. "Red," said Annie. "He's not fancy, and his name is Red."

Chapter Four

Annie looked at the clock. Five-thirty. Time to go. "Bye, Chels. Bye, Spunk-dog. Told my mom I'd be home before six o'clock." She raced out the door, put her foot in the stirrup, and swung her leg over Red, well, actually, her old red bike. Just then Chelsi's dad pulled his truck into the driveway. She waved wildly and pedaled off. Mr. Fidori was a nice man; he usually stopped to chat. Annie hoped he wouldn't mind that she messed up his newspaper.

Annie made a silent wish that Mr. Fidori wouldn't get laid off. It sounded bad. *Her* dad had a pretty safe job, even though they weren't rich. He was tired a lot from teaching and had lots of paperwork to do. Hopefully he would be in a good mood tonight.

Riding toward home, she wondered how she could bring up the subject of Red to her parents. Last time she mentioned getting a horse to her dad, he said it would happen *when hens crow*. Kind of like *when pigs fly*. He was always turning expressions around to say something silly, but to Annie this was a serious matter. Maybe if she surprised him with how much money she had stashed in the horse jar, her dad would be impressed. It wasn't enough to buy the whole horse, but maybe she could get a loan for the rest. She planned and schemed and rolled ideas around in her head all the way to the dinner table.

She watched as her dad spooned spaghetti onto his plate and her brother grabbed a piece of bread. She waited as her mom dished out the salad and passed the salad dressing. With food piled on her plate, she was too excited to even take one bite. She spit the words out before she lost her nerve entirely. "Mom, Dad, you know how I've been saving money to buy a horse for a really long time?"

A long quizzical look passed between her parents.

Mom broke the silence. "Yes, I know you have, honey."

Tyler kicked at Annie under the table. "Yeah, you wouldn't even let Mom borrow $20 from your horse money when she needed to go to the grocery store."

Annie slunk into her chair, cringing at the memory. She had felt stingy, greedy. She knew Mom would return the money. But Annie's number one rule for the horse jar was that nothing, *nada*, not one cent came out of it. It was there for one purpose only. To save for a horse.

"Yeah, like your *own* mother wasn't going to pay you back."

"Shut up, Tyler."

"That's done and over with now," said Mom. "Let's forget it ever happened."

Annie lost her train of thought. It was hard to get going again, but she tried.

"Well, I've found the most perfect horse," she said, knowing it sounded silly as soon as she said it. "His name is Red. Well, actually, I haven't seen him yet, but I know that he's the right one for me because of everything the lady told me on the phone . . ."

"He's the per-fect horse," Tyler sang out in a screechy voice. "But you've never even seen him?"

Annie continued, talking fast. "And . . . I've got more than half the money saved for him and I have a great plan for earning the rest. A lot of other people have called about this horse already, so I thought maybe we could make an appointment to look at him this weekend, and you could see how great he is, too, and then . . ."

"Whoa, back up there just a little bit, kiddo." Dad called everybody "kiddo." Kind of a silly name, but he meant well. But this time he wasn't in a joking mood. He started talking slowly, between bites of spaghetti, in a serious voice. "For starters, we don't really have any place to keep a horse."

Did this mean he was actually thinking about it? At least he hadn't said *when hens crow* or *when slugs swim*, or something impossible like that.

"And second of all," he went on, "do you have any idea how much it costs to take care of a horse?"

"Well, I figured we could keep him down at Cedar Grove Stables, and I could ride my bike over there every day and feed him."

"Every day? Before *and* after school? Even when it's raining?"

Annie hadn't really thought about that. It was so sunny out that it was hard to remember how hard it rained in winter.

"Do you know what it costs to keep a horse down at Cedar Grove?" Dad frowned. "Have you even thought about that? We just can't afford that right now."

This is not going well, thought Annie. She had been so sure of herself. She could already imagine riding Red around the arena at the stables.

"Paul," Mom broke in. "I think we need to hear Annie out. She's obviously given this a lot of thought."

Annie shot her mom a look of gratitude. She had planned

her speech so carefully, but now she felt tongue-tied.

"How much money have you saved, Annie?" Mom prompted.

"$528." Annie heard her dad take a quick breath.

"All by yourself?" he asked, as if he didn't believe her.

"Wow," said Tyler. "What did you do—rob a bank?"

"No, stupid. I've saved every penny that I've made working instead of spending it on dumb stuff. Remember when I helped Aunt Lou with our cousins last summer? She paid me a bunch for that, and I haven't spent any of it. And I took care of the Mendozas' animals when they went to Mexico—their chickens and those yappy Pomeranians. They're going again this summer. Last winter Mrs. Shelton paid me for helping her clean her garage, and I pulled weeds for the Jorgensons after all that rain we had. And when I'm thirteen, Mom says I can start babysitting."

Her words rushed out now. She had to say all of it. "I know I don't have the full amount, but if you guys could help out, I could cut ivy in the backyard for Mom, and maybe I can help Dad correct papers at night. I could pay you back in no time. Red sounds like a really good family horse, a good first horse. The lady that's selling him says he won't last long because there's a big demand for gentle horses. Can't we please just go look at him?"

Her dad cleared his throat. "Well, honey, it's pretty impressive that you've saved so much money."

Annie's heart did a double skip in her chest. Maybe this was the time. Maybe he finally saw . . .

"But look," he went on, "I know you kids. You think you want a horse. But it's just a phase. In a few years, you'll grow out of it."

"It's not a phase, Dad. It's all I ever think, hope, and dream about! Can't you understand that?" Annie's voice rose to a crescendo pitch.

But her dad got louder, too. "Annie, horses are a lot of trouble and expense. First of all, you'd have to pay big bucks down at that stable to keep it there. And then you'd have to buy a saddle and all kinds of other stuff that goes along with it. Then there are vet bills, and don't they need horseshoes, and who knows what else! We're not rich, Annie. If I were you, I'd save your money for something you'll *really* need someday, like a car, or going to college. Horses sound like a big waste of money to me."

"But Dad . . ."

"No buts about it. That's enough. Now let's just eat the rest of our dinner in peace."

Chapter Five

Annie couldn't eat. She felt like she was going to choke on her food. *Why doesn't Dad take me seriously?* she thought. *He treats me like I'm still a little girl, like I can't make any decisions for myself.* Annie forced down a few bites and asked to be excused from the table.

She crept up the stairs slowly and tucked herself into bed under her warm cotton quilt. *I know who I am. I know what I want.* She clenched her jaw, holding back the tears. She wouldn't cry. She wouldn't.

A little while later, she got up, pulled on her pajamas, brushed her teeth, and snuggled far back under the covers. Her brain was churning, plotting things out in her head.

She had to convince her dad that she could afford a horse. If it cost fifty dollars a month to keep a horse, she might be able to earn that much babysitting. It was almost summer, and then she could find other people besides the Mendozas who might need help taking care of their animals while on vacation. If she made up some business cards on the computer, she could pick up lots of work. Hopefully she could save enough money to keep her horse through the winter, when she would be back in school and might not be able to work as many odd jobs. Maybe she could get a part-time job after school when she got a little older.

What should I do first? Annie thought. She needed to make some phone calls to check out prices for boarding a horse. She hadn't really thought of that before. She just figured getting a horse would be easy, as soon as she had enough money to buy one.

As she lay there quietly, dreaming about a horse named Red with his elegant bay coat and black mane and tail, she heard the door open just a crack. A thin sliver of light from the hallway snuck through, and she recognized the slim figure of her mother standing there. "Honey, are you asleep?"

"No, Mom, you can come in."

"I just wanted to talk for a minute, okay?"

"Sure, talk away," said Annie. She wasn't really sleepy. She had too much on her mind.

Annie's mom sat on the edge of her bed. Everyone said they looked so much alike. Same brown hair, same brown eyes, even the same sprinkling of freckles over their nose. Now she spoke softly. "I just wanted to tell you, Annie, that I know how much getting a horse means to you. I know how hard you've been saving your money and how determined you are. And I wish that we lived farther out in the country, so that we had some land and a barn for you to keep a horse. Maybe someday. But right now, with only a teacher's income, we can't really afford it."

Annie nodded, blinking back a tear.

"I know how much you love horses. It's the only thing you ever look at when we drive out in the country."

Annie grinned. It was true. Mom liked to drag her along on her plant excursions. To nurseries filled with perennials, native plants, or roses. Annie would pull a red wagon up and down the aisles while her mom picked out plants. But Annie was waiting for the drive home. Meandering by pastures and fields, traveling down long lanes with cows and sheep bordering the roadways, Annie passed the time pressing her freckled nose hard against the car window, hoping to spot some horses.

Annie liked to imagine that she could pick the best one out of the whole herd. As the car made its way from fence line to fence line, her eyes would quickly scan the pastures, taking in all the colors, sizes, and breeds of horses, wondering what it would be like to own each one. Astride the palomino, she would be elegant. But the chestnut had longer legs and was probably faster. And the little paint pony looked like he was fun and friendly. Annie could look at horses for hours and hours. "I guess I have a one-track mind, huh?" she admitted.

"Well, you do tend to attack things with a certain passion." Her mom gave her a quick hug. "Maybe you and I are alike in that way."

"You know how you love plants and trees and flowers so much, and how they mean just about everything in the whole world to you?" Annie took a gulp of air, her words coming out too fast. "Well, that's how I feel about horses . . . "

Her mom was silent for a moment, as if gathering her thoughts. "I guess, Annie, what I came up here to tell you is that I know how much this means to you."

"Yeah, but Dad doesn't." Annie blurted it out, almost sobbing.

"Shhh, shhh." Annie's mother gathered her inside her strong arms, soothing her as if she were a small child.

Annie sucked her tears back inside. She quieted her

mind. She willed something to happen. Something good. Still, she could barely believe the words she heard next.

"I'll talk to your father. Maybe we can just go look at this horse to see what it's like, maybe get some ideas. Okay? Don't get your hopes up, though."

Annie tucked back under the blankets. She smiled to herself, and the smile went all the way from the top of her head down to the ends of her toes.

Chapter Six

This has to be the very best day of my life, thought Annie. Even better than the days spent at Cedar Grove Stables, riding the school horses around the arena. Annie couldn't imagine what her mother said to him, but Dad was actually driving the car to go look at a horse named Red.

Chelsi rode with her in the backseat with little Spunky snuggled between them. Annie hugged the dog against her, stroking his ears. Tyler was at a friend's birthday party. That was fine with Annie because she didn't want smarty-pants comments from her little brother spoiling such a special day.

"This doesn't mean we are *getting* a horse," Mr. Mitchell said, as they pulled out onto the freeway. "We are just going to go look at one." Yeah, yeah. Dads always have to act gruff. That's their job. But as they got closer, Annie crossed the fingers on both of her hands and kept them crossed. *I know something good will happen. I know something good will happen.* She kept repeating it silently to herself. Maybe the more she said it, the more likely it was to happen.

Annie's heart thumped in her chest as they turned down a long gravel drive lined with pastures. Spunky licked her face, as if catching the excitement.

The car stopped in front of a modest barn. Annie spied a well-tended mobile home, with several corrals and a small riding ring alongside it. Chickens scratched in the gravel, and in front of the barn was a wooden hitching rail. Tied there, with a nylon lead, was a bright bay horse. He stood quietly except for his tail, which occasionally swished at a fly. A middle-aged lady was brushing him, and his coat shone the color of a brand-new penny.

The lady turned with a smile and began walking toward them. As Annie emerged from the car, blinking in the sun, she was met with a handshake. "You must be Annie," said the lady. "My name is Terry, and this here is Red." She untied Red and started walking him around for everyone to see.

Annie was so nervous she could barely move her legs. The horse was perfect, just like she had dreamed. Not too big. Not too fancy. Just a nice plain bay horse.

Annie's dad came around the side of the car. "We're the Mitchells," he said, reaching out his hand as the woman walked close. "We're not sure . . ."

But he was cut off in mid-sentence. Spunky leaped out of Chelsi's arms, running to smell the strange animal towering above him. "Spunk, come back here," Chelsi cried. Before she could reach him, Red extended his long neck and, with delicate nostrils, examined Spunky all over. Then Red blew through his nostrils, in a horsey expression of satisfaction and approval.

"I think Red likes him," said Chelsi.

"Yep. This horse definitely likes dogs as well as people. He's just an all-around unflappable kind of horse," said Terry.

After that, everything seemed like a dream. Red stood

quietly while Terry cleaned his hooves and saddled him. She led the horse around a bit, showing Annie how to check his cinch and make sure it was tight enough to hold the saddle while she mounted. Annie was nervous with everyone watching, but she remembered how to squeeze her legs and cluck softly to prompt Red to go forward. He moved as if he could read her mind. When she asked him to stop, she remembered what she had learned during her riding lessons— how to lean back and set her weight down on the saddle, say *whoa*, and then check the horse with the reins. Red was perfect! She rode him in a figure eight around the ring, then outside the ring on the driveway, and eventually back inside. Red did everything she asked.

"He certainly seems to respond well," said Annie's dad.

"Well, this horse was a 4-H show horse when he was younger. Plus he's been on lots and lots of trails with kids. He loads in a horse trailer with absolutely no problem and, to my knowledge, he's as sound as a dollar," said Terry. "I know he's older, but a horse this age is the kind that you want to get your daughter started with. He's what you call a 'been there, done that' kind of horse. Good kids' horses are hard to find, and they are worth their weight in gold. I've had a lot of calls on him, and I'm sure he'll go fast, now that summer is almost here."

Terry's sales pitch sounded good to Annie. She thought of the fancy horse jar sitting on her shelf, holding all of her hard-earned dimes, nickels, and dollars, along with all of her dreams, hopes, and wishes. She was ready to put all of her money down right on the spot. She looked over at her parents, trying to gather some clue as to what they were thinking. Her mother had a guarded smile on her face. Her dad stood with his arms folded across his chest. *Oh, please!*

Oh, please! thought Annie. She sat quietly on the bay gelding's back. But she wanted to jump for joy, to assure her parents that if they could just loan her the rest of the money to buy Red, *the most perfect horse*, she would work hard to pay them back as quick as she could.

Chelsi broke the spell. "Does he ride double?" she asked.

"Oh, you betcha. You just climb right up there," said Terry. And with that, she kind of half-boosted, half-lifted Chelsi up onto Red's back, behind Annie. Then Terry called Spunky over to her and lifted him up onto the saddle in front of the two girls. "See, this horse even rides triple." Annie and Chelsi laughed, and the three of them took a slow walk around the ring, as if to prove the point.

It looked as if Annie's dad was won over. As Red made another circle and stopped in front of him, he stroked the soft nose of the red gelding tentatively. Annie's mom, who had hardly said a word the whole time, beamed up at Annie. Mr. Mitchell finally spoke up. "This does seem like a nice horse," he said.

Annie's heart did a complete loop-de-loop in her chest. It was happening! It was happening! Her very own horse. Her first, real, honest-to-goodness horse.

"But I'm afraid we just don't have anywhere to keep him at the moment."

No! Annie couldn't believe her ears. "What about down at Cedar Grove?" she blurted out. She had checked on the boarding stables, and they had space available. Kind of pricey, but . . .

"We actually called down there, honey," said her mom, in a soft voice. "It's just way too expensive."

"But I'll get a job," cried Annie. Chelsi slid off Red's back, landing with a thump on the ground. Spunk-dog jumped into her arms, while Red stood absolutely still. Annie stayed where she was, seated tightly on the gentle horse's back.

"Look, this is a very nice horse," Annie's dad said. He turned to Terry. "I really appreciate your time in showing him to us. Even though my daughter has worked diligently and saved her money, I don't feel we're quite ready for a horse. Boarding is more expensive than I ever anticipated."

Annie looked around the yard wildly. How could she be so close to her dream, but just out of reach? She spied the flock of chickens, moving closer now, pecking at bugs on the short grass growing near the barn. They looked like hens. She didn't see any throwing back their heads to crow. As if *that* was going to happen. Annie put her foot in the stirrup, lowered herself off Red's broad back, and slunk to the backseat of the car, barely containing her tears.

Chapter Seven

Annie thought Monday would never end. She had a hard time concentrating in school. She almost didn't hear her teacher, Mrs. Finley, call for library books. "Annie, did you take your books up to the book crate? We have library second period."

"Yeah, Annie. We know you *always* have horse books," teased Justin, the boy who sat behind her.

Justin's sarcastic comments drove Annie nuts. Not to mention how his overgrown brown hair practically covered his eyes, which were actually a dark blue, when Annie could see them.

"Well, so what! At least I *read*." Annie always felt like she had to make some smart reply back to Justin. She didn't know why. He irritated her. And she wasn't having a good day. She couldn't help wondering if someone else had bought Red. She had spent Sunday moping around the house, thinking of ways to convince her parents that she could afford a horse. What was the use? Especially when she remembered what her dad had said earlier, that horses were just a "phase" she was going through.

Mrs. Finley led the class down the hallway. They waited,

in single file with their voices turned off, for the librarian, Mrs. Griffen, to tell them it was okay to come into the library. Justin and a few of the other boys continued to make smart remarks, just under their breath, and shoved each other when the teacher wasn't looking. *They are so immature*, thought Annie. As they filed into the library, Mrs. Griffen had some news for Annie. "We just cataloged two brand-new horse books," she told her. "I've been saving them for you."

Mrs. Griffen was a great librarian. She liked horses, too. Annie thought she knew by heart most of the horse books in the library, but Mrs. Griffen always seemed to find another one to display on the top shelves just before their class came in. But today books weren't enough for Annie.

"Thanks," she said, half-heartedly.

"Why so down in the mouth?" asked Mrs. Griffen. "I thought you'd be excited."

"I guess I'm tired of just reading about horses. I want one of my own so badly."

Justin interrupted. "Why would anyone want a horse?" he said. "I'd much rather have a motorcycle. They go *fast*. Faster than a dumb horse could ever go."

"Oh, why don't you just shut up, Justin," Annie snapped. Before she could think about it, she put her arm out and slightly pushed him.

Justin made a face, sticking out his big tongue and looking ugly.

"Annie. Justin. Over here right now!" Mrs. Finley shouted in her mean voice. "That is not appropriate library behavior! Sit in those two chairs right there, and you may sit there for the rest of the library period."

Annie was mortified. She had never been in trouble in

the library, not in her entire life. She put her head down on her hands to hide her face. Justin chuckled as he sat down. Annie glanced up to see three or four other boys laughing, too, as if they were glad it wasn't them. They thought it was funny. Annie didn't think so. Now she probably wouldn't be able to check out the new horse books Mrs. Griffen had saved for her. She'd probably never get a *real* horse, either.

"Hey, Annie," Justin whispered.

"Shh, we'll get in more trouble."

"No, we won't. Look," said Justin. He pointed toward the door. Mrs. Finley was headed to the staff room, coffee cup in hand, for a break. "Hey, I wanted to tell you something. About the horse you want to get."

"What about it?" Annie was not feeling very friendly toward Justin at the moment.

"Do you know where the Mendozas live, at the end of Walker Lane, right by you?"

"Yeah," said Annie. She knew exactly where the Mendozas lived. She had ridden her bike there twice a day last summer, taking care of their pets and garden while they visited family in Mexico. She even knew exactly how long it took to get there from her house—five minutes.

"Well, right next to their house, there's a sign in a big field. It says, 'Pasture for Rent—$25 a month'," said Justin.

"What?" Annie was amazed. "You mean the field between the Mendozas and the blue house?"

"Yeah, that's the one. I was down there yesterday on my bike, just riding around. I was waiting to tell you today."

Excitement pulsed through Annie's body. Her brain perked up and began turning possibilities around and around. She peeked her head up to see if the class was lining up.

"Thanks, Justin." She meant it. It pained her to be nice

to him after he had been such a pest, but this was the best news she had received all day. A place to keep a horse. It seemed to Annie that whenever things looked really bad, there was always something around the corner, sometimes surprising things, that made everything better.

Chapter Eight

Annie parked her bike and peered over the fence. The field on Walker Lane was overgrown with tall grass, thistles, and weeds, and littered with old cans and bottles. The wire fence was sagging and broken in spots. It didn't look like a very safe place for Red, or any horse.

Mr. Mendoza's car pulled up alongside her. "Hey there, Annie-girl. You going to put an animal in here?"

"I'd like to. I've been looking at a horse that's for sale. But this pasture doesn't look too safe."

"You're right about that. The people that own it live out of town, and they haven't been here in years. But they asked me to put the sign up and try to get it rented."

"I was excited about it until I saw it," said Annie, her shoulders slumping. "My dad says we can't afford to board a horse at the stable, and this sounded pretty reasonable. But it looks like a lot of work," said Annie.

"Well, you're a hardworking girl," Mr. Mendoza chuckled. "And it looks like help just showed up." He winked.

Annie glanced over her shoulder at another bike coming down the lane. It was Justin!

"What are you doing here?" she asked. *Try to be nice,* she

told herself. *He's the one that told you about the pasture.*

"I just wanted to see what you thought. Kind of a mess, huh?" Justin laid his bike down in the ditch. He picked up a piece of sagging barbed wire, stretching it tight. "But we could fix this up. Just pull this over and nail it up good. There's a couple of places on the other side that we better check, too."

"We?" Annie smiled halfway, unsure.

Mr. Mendoza spoke up. "I'll get you kids some nails and a hammer. You just go right ahead and fix all you want."

Annie shaded her eyes from the sun, studying the middle of the field. "What about all that trash out there?"

"If you make a pile out here by the road, you can throw it all in my Dumpster," said Mr. Mendoza. "I'd like to see something out here to eat this pasture. Keep it cleaned up."

Annie followed Mr. Mendoza back to his house to get a hammer and nails. She was almost in a state of shock thinking about Justin's offer to help, but she was in no position to refuse. She asked to borrow the telephone. "Mom," she said. "I'm over at Mr. Mendoza's, working on a project." She didn't tell her mom about the pasture. She wanted it to be a surprise.

As Mr. Mendoza and Annie walked back toward the toolshed, they passed the chicken coop. He had banty chickens, as well as some big, red laying hens.

"Do hens ever crow?" she asked, hoping she didn't sound too silly.

"You wouldn't think so, would you? But a couple of times in my life, I've seen a young hen actually trying to crow. I've always thought they were a little mixed up. But then maybe no one told them that they couldn't, and they just had a lot of try in them. Like you, young lady. You're quite a go-getter."

Annie blushed. She felt like throwing her head back and crowing herself, but she was too bashful. Besides, Justin might hear. She could see him studying the fence, absorbed in the job ahead of him. Suddenly she thought of something else important.

"Where would the horse drink?" she asked. "It's going to need water."

"Well, if you're ready for another big job, I've got something you could use."

Annie followed him, poking through the high weeds that bordered the pasture. When they came to a halt, there—filled with mud and green algae and almost hidden from view—was an old porcelain bathtub.

"It came out of the house when we remodeled. If you want to use it for a watering trough, we could run a hose over to it from my garden faucet."

"It's filthy." Annie wrinkled her nose. "I guess I could clean it up, though."

Annie scrubbed the old bathtub until her hands were red and raw. She kept imagining Red dipping his head into the fresh water, enjoying a long, cool drink. As she glanced up into the pasture, pushing her hair back out of her face, she saw Justin making progress on the fence. She could almost envision her horse (*her* horse, she knew it would be true) walking the fence line, investigating his new domain.

The project took longer than they expected. What looked like a simple afternoon's work actually took them three whole days after school. It went faster when Chelsi came to help. They hauled garbage, cans, and old rusty wire, placing them by the road and later loading them into the Dumpster. Mr. Mendoza even helped them build a

simple, three-sided shelter out of plywood and shingles he had laying around in his yard. Spunky was right under their feet the whole time. He had to be in the middle of everything.

"What kind of dog *is* that?" asked Justin, as they were finishing for the day.

"Everybody always asks," said Chelsi. "He's registered. A wire-haired dachshund."

"Yeah, he's got weird hair, all right," said Justin. "No offense, but he looks like a mutt."

Annie smirked, glancing at Chelsi.

"Yeah, I know," said Chelsi. "But we love him anyway. Don't we, Spunk-dog?" Chelsi loaded Spunky into the basket of her bike, preparing to ride him home.

"Hey, I gotta take off," said Justin, wheeling his bike around to face them. "My parents said I better really get on my homework, since I've been over here so much."

Annie didn't know what to say to Justin. He was the one who had spotted the pasture in the first place, and his help was more than she ever expected. "Thanks a whole bunch," she spit out, a little embarrassed. "See you at school."

"Yup. See ya." He pointed at Chelsi's bike as he pedaled away. "Hey, Chelsi. Your tire is flat."

"Darn it," said Chelsi. "I knew it was low on air, but I didn't want to ask my dad to fix it."

"How come?" asked Annie.

"He got a pink slip from work."

Annie shoved the last armload of cans into the Dumpster. "What's that?"

Chelsi looked down, not meeting Annie's glance. "It means he got laid off. I heard my parents talking, well, kind of shouting. It means we can't afford our rent now, or our truck payment, or anything."

"Oh, no. I'm sorry," said Annie. That didn't sound good. "Well, thanks for helping with the pasture, Chels. You too, Spunk." She ruffled the little dog's head.

"Yeah, it was actually sort of fun. Good luck talking to your dad." Chelsi walked down the lane slowly, balancing the bike with the flat tire and her dog.

Annie felt bad for her friend. She wished there was something she could do to help. But right now, she had to concentrate on the problem in front of her. Now that the pasture was ready for Red, she had to figure out the best way to approach her dad.

Chapter Nine

Red was still available. Annie had called every evening, just to make sure.

"I can't believe I haven't sold him yet," said Terry. "He must be waiting for you to come get him."

"Well, maybe we will soon," said Annie.

Now what should she say to her dad? He knew nothing about the pasture or all the hard work she had been doing. Then Tyler almost spilled the beans.

"Annie's been over on Walker Lane every day," he said at dinner. "With a boy!"

Had Tyler been spying on her? Little brothers were such a pain. Annie kicked him hard under the table. But she had to think fast to head this one off. "Justin's been working, doing some stuff on the field next to Mr. Mendoza's," she said. Which was true. "And I rode my bike over there to watch." Which was also true.

Her mother and father exchanged one of those long, knowing glances across the dinner table. They did that a lot lately. Annie kept her hands in her lap, hoping they wouldn't notice how raw they were from working.

Then they changed the subject, and nothing more was

said.

By the next afternoon, the pasture was finally finished. Annie raced her bike up the driveway, rehearsing what she wanted to say to her dad. Just as she reached the garage, she heard the purr of a familiar motor. Her dad was home from work, earlier than usual.

"Wow, you're a mess. Looks like you've been collecting garbage or something. Where ya' been, kiddo?"

This was it. Her big moment. At the last second, Annie decided that the truth was the best way to go. So she just spit it out.

"I found a pasture for rent. It's over on Walker Lane. It's only $25 a month, and it takes me five minutes to ride my bike over there." The words escaped quickly now. "Justin and I have been cleaning it. Chelsi helped, too. Mr. Mendoza loaned us wood, nails, and a hammer, and there was a ton of trash out in the middle of it. We got it all cleaned up. And I scrubbed and scrubbed to make this old bathtub useable, and . . ."

Her dad held his hand up like a crossing guard directing traffic, stopping her in mid-sentence. "Let me get this straight," he said. "You've been doing all of this, hoping that you might still get that horse?"

"Red," she said. "He's still available. I called."

"You know, you've got a little stubborn streak in you, kiddo. When you get a hold of something, you don't know how to let it go. Kind of like a dog worrying a bone." He grinned. "You're just like your mother in that respect."

"Mr. Mendoza said that he'd like to have an animal in there to eat the pasture down," she continued, hoping for a miracle.

"Your mother and I have been tossing this thing back

and forth all week," he said, pushing the kitchen door open. He set his briefcase down, which was filled with papers that he brought home from school. "Is your homework all done?"

"I finished it all in school."

"Well, how would you like to help me correct some social studies tests?" he asked.

"Sure, Dad," answered Annie.

"Your mother kind of made me see the light. She said that it's a shame to let all of your hard work go unrewarded. That you're a good student, and you've never given us a lick of trouble, and that you seem to want this more than anything else in the world."

Annie nodded, not believing what she was hearing. "More than anything at all."

"Well, one of the things that concerns me is your safety. A horse is a very large animal, and I worry about you being out there in the pasture with it, all by yourself. But Mr. Mendoza is retired, and he seems to be home most of the time. If he could just look over the fence and check on you from time to time, it would be a big relief to me."

Tears were bright in Annie's eyes. Was she hearing this right?

"And another thing," he continued. "The woman that is selling that horse."

"Her name is Terry," Annie choked out. "And the horse's name is Red."

"Right. Well, maybe we could ask Terry to come over and give you some initial lessons on the horse. Get everyone situated in their new surroundings. What do you think of that idea?"

Annie thought it was a brilliant idea. Only she didn't say so. She couldn't get any words out at all without sounding like a blubbering baby. She just nodded.

"Well, go get that jar of yours," her dad said. "If you're ready to buy a horse, it's going to take all the money you've got in that thing. We'll help you out with the rest of it, but you're going to have to pull a lot of weeds for your mother, and correct a lot of papers for me to make up for it. Are you ready for this?"

Was he kidding? Annie had been waiting her entire life for this moment. She bolted up the stairs to retrieve the horse jar.

Chapter Ten

Now the details of owning a horse became real for her. Annie emptied the horse jar, counting every hard-earned dollar and cent that she had saved. When she took the money over as a deposit, Terry offered to throw in Red's bridle, as well as a halter and a lead rope. But Annie still needed to buy a saddle and blanket, brushes, and a hoof pick.

So she made some business cards on the computer.

Hard worker will take care of your animals,
do yardwork, and other odd jobs.
Need money to pay for horse.

There, that said it all. Annie ran her fingers over the muscles in her arms. She was getting strong. She would have to work hard to pay her parents back and get the things she needed for Red.

Everything was set. Terry would bring the bay gelding in a horse trailer next weekend. Annie didn't know how she could wait that long. She began counting down the days. *Only three more days without a horse*, she said to herself, over and over, as the big day drew closer. Then, *only two more days.* She dreamed of pedaling her bike to the pasture every day, where Red would greet her with a nicker. She pictured the bright red horse stretching his neck over the fence, awaiting her arrival. She would brush Red until he shone. Then she would pull herself up onto his broad back, and . . .

"Annie, get up. You're going to be late for school if you stay in bed any longer." Her mother's voice drifted up the stairs. Annie tried to wake up, but her eyes wouldn't open. Finally, she remembered. *This is the last day of my life that I will be without a horse.*

Annie swung her feet slowly to the floor. Still in her pajamas, she drifted sleepy-eyed to the breakfast table.

"It's been declared a noxious weed in this state!" Mrs. Mitchell announced loudly.

"What has?" said Annie. The newspaper was spread out all over the kitchen table, and Mom was getting more excited by the minute.

"Ivy. English ivy. I knew it was a pest. It kills trees, and now they've declared it a weed. Now they won't be able to sell it at nurseries anymore. A weed! Just like I've always suspected."

Annie was still lost in her daydream about Red. She wasn't really thinking about ivy. "Chelsi and I are going to ride our bikes over to the pasture after school. We're going to check one last time and make sure everything is perfect. Is that okay?" She poured cereal into a bowl, smothered it with milk, and shoveled it down. She had to hurry and get her bike out of the garage. She didn't want to be late riding with Chelsi to school.

"Okay, honey. Thanks for letting me know. I know you're excited about tomorrow."

Annie practically ran to the garage. She almost forgot her

book bag. She strapped the bag on her back, pushed her bike out the side door, and pedaled hard toward Chelsi's house. She stopped dreaming about Red for just a moment and thought about Chelsi's problems. *What if Chelsi's dad couldn't find another job, and they had to move?* That would be awful. Chelsi was her best friend in the whole world, and she was looking forward to spending the summer with Chelsi, Spunky, and Red. Maybe Justin would even want to ride Red around the pasture. Would she let him?

As she got close to Chelsi's house, she saw her friend was on foot, just closing the gate to the backyard.

"Stay there, Spunky," said Chelsi. "He'd better stay. My dad never put up an electric wire fence. And my bike tire is still flat," she said. "Come on, we've got to hurry. I'll run."

Annie stood on the pedals, pumping hard, as Chelsi trotted alongside. They crossed busy Second Street with barely a nod at the cars rushing by. Then they turned onto Conners Way toward school. For some reason, Annie looked back. Something clicked in her brain like a snapshot—a memory of a small, short-legged dog running for all he was worth, trying to catch up.

As Annie slowed her bike, Chelsi turned, too. Spunky was on the far edge of Second Street, coming at a full gallop. Chelsi hollered at her dog. "No, Spunky. Stay! Stay there!"

But the little dachshund charged straight ahead, looking neither left or right.

"No, Spunky! No!" Annie and Chelsi screamed in unison. Everything seemed to slow down. Just like watching a scary movie in slow motion—no matter how awful, it still plays out, and there's nothing that can be done to change the outcome.

Annie heard the cars honking, but Spunky kept running.

When all was quiet again, Spunky was lying totally still in the middle of the road. A man got out of his car. Annie dropped her bike, sprinting with Chelsi towards the dog.

"I'm so sorry," the man said. He stood in the middle of the road, diverting traffic. "He ran right out in front of me. I couldn't stop in time."

Annie had her arm around her friend's shoulder. She could barely bring herself to look at Spunky, and she wasn't sure what to do.

"Is there a veterinarian around here?" said the man.

"Is he dead? Is he dead?" sobbed Chelsi.

"Dr. Cooper is right up the road." Annie's mother walked up quickly. She held a bag containing Annie's lunch, left behind on the kitchen counter. Annie's mom dropped to her knees on the pavement and put her hand against the dog. "He's still breathing. I've got an old blanket in the trunk of my car. Maybe we can get him onto that."

Gently, the adults slid the dog onto the blanket and lifted him into the backseat. Mrs. Mitchell drove the short distance to the veterinarian's office, while Annie and Chelsi sat huddled in front. Annie's mom dashed into the reception area, and soon Dr. Cooper and two employees hurried out to the car. Picking the blanket up carefully, they rushed Spunky inside.

Annie followed, with her arm around Chelsi, who was shaking all over. It smelled strange in the vet's office, like strong antiseptic mixed with doggie odor. Annie glanced at the wall as she led Chelsi down the hallway. Dr. Cooper's name was displayed prominently in framed awards. She hoped that meant he was a good doctor. He had to save Spunky. He just had to.

In the examination room, Annie and Chelsi slid through

the door and stood next to Annie's mother. Spunky lay sideways on a steel table. Dr. Cooper was pressing him gently all over. Spunky didn't move at all. It was hard to tell if he was dead or alive.

Dr. Cooper's mouth was pressed tight, and he was shaking his head. "Well, his back leg is broken. Perhaps in more than one place. We're going to need to x-ray it. He appears to have internal injuries, too. I can't guarantee his chances, but we can certainly try. Would you like me to proceed?"

Mrs. Mitchell cleared her throat. "He's not really our dog. He belongs to the Fidoris." She glanced around at Chelsi. "Are they home, honey?"

Chelsi shook her head. "Dad said he's going to be gone all day. He's putting in job applications. Mom went with him. She's looking for a job, too."

"Is there a phone number where they can be reached?"

Chelsi looked down. "No. Not until they get back."

Dr. Cooper spoke kindly to Chelsi. "We'll take your dog into the back and give him some pain medication. But we would like to operate soon, if that's what you decide."

Annie looked over at her friend. Tears dribbled down Chelsi's cheek.

Annie's mother spoke up. "I'll get you the Fidoris' home number."

Chapter Eleven

Annie's mother drove the girls back to school. Annie retrieved her bike from where she had left it in the street and parked it in the bike rack. "Spunky's in good hands," her mom said, as she signed a late notice for both of them. "There's nothing more we can do right now."

But Annie couldn't concentrate in class. She kept thinking of the little Spunk-dog lying injured and all alone in a cold steel cage.

At lunchtime, Chelsi and Annie sat huddled over their sandwiches, too worried to enjoy their food. Justin came by their table and asked what was the matter. "Chelsi's dog got hit by a car this morning, and he's at the vet's office," said Annie. She looked over at Chelsi, who blinked back tears, almost choking on her sandwich.

"Oh, man, that's too bad. He's a pretty cute little dog. Hope he makes it." And with that, Justin was out the door to play soccer with his friends.

"I do, too," mumbled Annie, to nobody in particular.

After school, Annie pedaled home slowly. Chelsi walked beside her in almost total silence. Nothing they could say to each other would take away the worry. Annie's excitement over picking up her horse was suddenly on a back burner. It seemed unimportant compared to poor Spunky.

Nobody was home yet at the Fidoris' house. Annie watched her friend unlock the front door and wave a sad goodbye.

Annie hoped Chelsi's parents would get home soon. They needed to talk to the vet about what could be done for Spunky. She hoped it was good news, so that tomorrow could be a happy day—the day she was finally getting her very own horse.

But it was not good news. When the phone rang later that afternoon, Chelsi was crying. Crying so hard that Annie could barely make out the words.

"Chelsi, what is it?" asked Annie. "Talk slower. What happened? What did your parents say?"

Chelsi blubbered like a baby. "My dad. He said we can't afford it right now. Because, because he doesn't have a job." Chelsi's words came out in bursts between sobs. "The vet said it's going to cost a lot of money to operate on Spunky because he needs pins in his legs or something. It's going to cost several hundred dollars. My dad said, he said, we can't spend that kind of money right now. He said we have to put Spunky to sleep."

"What??" *To sleep?* Annie was shocked into silence. Usually she had an answer for everything, but now she was practically speechless. "Oh, Chels, I'm sorry." She hung up the phone. Her mind was working—spinning in circles—trying to come up with a plan. She thought about Spunky, money, and about how just when everything seemed perfect, suddenly everything was awful. She couldn't think anymore. Her head hurt. She needed to get out in the air and sort things out.

Annie left her mom a note and took off on her bike. She had no particular destination. She just needed to be outside. Instead of heading towards Red's pasture, she pedaled down the hill toward the river. She remembered how Spunky had raced to catch up with them when he dug out of his pen the first time. Would his tiny legs ever run that fast again?

Annie couldn't bear to think of Spunky lying there in the vet's office, injured, in pain, and awaiting his fate. *Put to sleep.* She knew what those words meant. They were a grown-up's way of glossing over the actual event. Annie had asked her mom one time what "put to sleep" really meant. And her mom had given her an honest answer. Annie was thankful for that, so she knew the real situation. She knew those innocent-sounding words really meant putting a needle in the vein of little Spunky's leg and giving him a shot that would let him die without pain. *Die.* It was a word that Annie couldn't fathom. She knew everything died eventually—all people, all animals. But not Spunk-dog. He didn't deserve to die.

Annie's mind was a wild tangle of thoughts, racing through her brain in all kinds of patterns. Pedaling her bike along the river road, she noticed a small trail leading through the underbrush, slanting toward the water. She got off her bike and dropped it sideways into the weeds.

The bank was steep, and she slid down, scooting all the way to the bottom. Sheltered by a deep canopy of maples, ferns, and tall fir, she sat at the very edge of the restless water. Two mallards arose from the shallows, so close that she heard their wings beat as they flew overhead.

she said to herself, *just one more day.*

But it was no use. Her mind kept filling with pictures of a small dog lying still in the street, and then on the cold steel table in Dr. Cooper's office. Annie knew there was an answer, if she could only come across it.

Annie sat very still on the bank of the river—listening and waiting. All she heard was the wind. It began as a rustle far downstream, where the water ran under the bridge near town. It gathered energy as it moved upstream to where Annie sat, in the agony of uncertainty. As the wind moved briskly up the river, it seemed to pick up Annie's thoughts and plans, as if they were leaves from the trees. It blew them around and around, shuffling and scattering them in a random fashion.

As the wind finally died back down, Annie's hopes and dreams and schemes all settled into a different design. Annie suddenly knew what she must do. She clambered up the river bank, pulled her bike from the bushes, and pedaled quickly up the hill toward home, sure in her decision.

Chapter Twelve

"Mom, I need to make a phone call. I need your help!" Annie burst into the house. Her bike lay in a heap by the front door, and her sneakers were muddy from her trip to the river's edge. But it didn't matter. Time was important now. She had to hurry!

"Hi, honey. I've been wondering when you'd get home. I found your note," said Annie's mom.

Tyler wandered about the living room, crinkling the newspaper in his hands.

"Move, Tyler." She almost ran him over. "Out of my way."

"Geez. I was just looking through the ads for you. I thought you might be interested." His shoulders moved up and down uncertainly. "Here's a new one. It says, 'Used Saddle—$125.'"

"Not now, Tyler. I don't have time." She brushed him aside. "Mom, where's Terry's phone number? The lady who has Red?" Annie had called the number so often she knew it by heart, but her head was spinning so fast she couldn't remember it.

Annie's mother found the number on the counter. Annie grabbed it impatiently. She didn't mean to be rude, but she

couldn't help it. She had to make this phone call, and quickly.

"Hello, Terry? This is Annie Mitchell—you know the girl who is buying Red?" Annie saw her mother's puzzled face, as she listened to the conversation.

"I know you are planning to deliver him tomorrow morning. I'm very sorry, but I need to get my deposit back." The money that came out of her horse jar. *$528*, Annie thought. A lump formed at the back of her throat, but she ignored it. "I'm not going to be able to buy him after all. We have an emergency. I mean, my friend's dog has an emergency." Annie quickly explained the story about what had happened to Spunky.

"Well," said Terry slowly, "usually a deal is a deal."

Annie's heart flip-flopped. What if she couldn't get her money back?

"But this does sound like an unusual circumstance." Terry paused, as if thinking it over. "I thought Red would be a great horse for you, but I have somebody else who's very interested in him also. I'll give him a call right now."

Annie sucked in her breath. "Okay," she said.

"Why don't you have your parents bring you over this weekend to get your money back. I'm real sorry, honey."

"Me, too," Annie mumbled. But she couldn't think about sorry right now. She turned to her mother again. "Can you find Dr. Cooper's number for me?"

Annie glanced up and noticed the front door pushed open. Standing squarely in the middle was her father, looking baffled. Had he heard the conversation? "What's going on?" he asked.

Annie looked straight at her dad for a moment, then averted her eyes. Here she was, changing her mind about the horse, just like he had predicted. What would he think of her now?

As her mother pointed to a page in the directory, Annie punched the numbers into the phone. Her fingers trembled, and she was afraid she would lose her nerve.

"Dr. Cooper's office. Can we help you?"

Annie could hear dogs barking in the background. "Yes, ma'am. This is Annie Mitchell. And I want to make sure that Chelsi's little dog, Spunky, is still alive."

"Oh, the little dachshund? You mean the Fidoris' dog? Well, yes, he's still back there in a cage. He has a broken leg, I believe, but he's not in any pain. He was sedated after the accident. But the family doesn't seem to have the money, and we . . ."

"Well, you're not going to put him to sleep!" Annie practically screamed into the phone. She tried to steady her voice. "I have the money for his operation. Well, actually, I'll have it tomorrow, as soon as I get the deposit for my horse back. But we'll come down right now and make the arrangements. I can pay for it. I want to."

"All right. I'll tell the doctor as soon as I can. We're pretty busy here right now."

Annie hung up the phone. Her whole body was shaking. There. It was done.

Her father was looking at her in a strange way. "You've changed your mind about Red?"

Annie nodded her head glumly, unable to meet his eye now. She glanced up at her mother, looking for support. Annie's mother just had a small, pinched smile on her face. "I'll get my jacket," is all she said.

They drove in silence to Dr. Cooper's office. Annie sat in the back with Tyler, keeping her thoughts to herself. As they

63

pulled into the parking lot, Annie's father turned toward the backseat. "Annie, this is a very big decision you are making. You have planned and saved for a horse for an awfully long time. I hate to see you throw it all away in a hasty decision. Are you sure this is what you want to do with your money?"

"Yes," said Annie, in a strong voice. "I'm sure."

Her dad cleared his throat. "I'm very proud of you, Annie. No matter what decision you make."

Annie swallowed hard. Her dad was proud of her!

She opened the door to the veterinarian's office. The waiting room overflowed with people and animals, and she had to wait her turn. A woman held a large Siamese cat. A small boy was being dragged around the office by a gangly golden retriever on a leash.

The lady behind the desk was doing her best to help everyone, but Annie was becoming impatient. She stood on one foot, and then the other. Finally, sliding up to the counter, her words came out in a rush. "Hello. I'm Annie Mitchell. I called, remember? My friend Chelsi and I were here this morning when Spunk-dog—I mean, her dog, Spunky—got run over . . . and, well, could I speak to Dr. Cooper? It's very important! He can't put Spunky to sleep because I was going to buy a horse, but now I'm not, and I have the money—I mean . . ." Annie stopped. "I will have the money as soon as I get my deposit back. Can you tell me how much it will be to pay Spunky's bill?"

"Well, I don't know. The dog's injuries are rather extensive, and there would be a charge for the anesthetic, the operation, and the . . ."

Annie didn't notice Dr. Cooper coming out of one of the examination rooms. "Did I hear my name being called?"

"Yes, doctor. This young lady is interested in how much

it would cost to operate on the dachshund back there, the one that was hit by a car this morning."

"I was here this morning when we brought Spunky in. Do you remember?" asked Annie.

Dr. Cooper looked up from the chart he was carrying. "You were here with your friend, right?"

"Yes. I'm Annie Mitchell, and I was going to buy a horse." Annie's words gushed out. "I put down a deposit of $528, which was all the money I had in my horse jar, but the lady I'm buying him from said she'd refund the money since it's an emergency. I was wondering, will that be enough to fix Spunky?"

Dr. Cooper's eyebrows came together as if he was thinking, trying to figure this out. "Now let me understand this correctly," he said. "The little dog back there doesn't even belong to you, is that right?"

"Well, he actually belongs to my best friend, Chelsi Fidori. But he's a great dog, and he loves us both. He likes to go with us all the time. In fact, that's how he got run over. He was trying to follow us to school," said Annie.

"But this money that you want to pay me, it was money you were saving to buy a horse?"

Annie's mother, who had been strangely quiet all this time, suddenly stepped forward. "That's right, Dr. Cooper. Annie has been working very hard and saving all her money. She has wanted a horse for as long as she could remember. She finally convinced her father, and we found a nice, gentle horse to buy. He was going to be delivered tomorrow. But that was before Spunky got hurt, and now she has decided this is what she wants to do with her money. It's her own choice."

"Please, Dr. Cooper." Annie wiped a tear from the corner

65

of her eye. "I want you to make Spunky better. He's a good dog, and we love him."

"And does your friend Chelsi know that you are doing this?"

"No, but it doesn't matter. I mean, it's my money, and I want to pay for this operation to fix his leg. But do I have enough money?"

Dr. Cooper pursed his lips, as if trying to take all of this in. "Well, young lady, I think maybe we can work something out. Let me just get some information down here. I'll call the Fidoris to get their permission, and we can probably set that little dog's leg tonight."

Chapter Thirteen

Annie didn't know how she was going to make it through the weekend. The hours just seemed to drag. Her mother and father made the trip back to Terry's barn to get the deposit back. Annie stayed home. She couldn't bear to see the bright bay horse again, the one that was almost hers. She asked her parents if they would take the money to the animal hospital to pay for Spunky's operation. She knew she was making a good decision. Spunky was still alive, and that was all that mattered. So then why did she have such a hollow place in the pit of her stomach?

On Saturday afternoon, the doorbell rang. Annie peeked out the window. Chelsi stood on the front porch, looking nervous. "Hi," she said, when Annie opened the door.

"Hey," said Annie. She looked down at her feet, unsure of what to say next. It felt like there was an invisible wall between them.

"Spunky's going to be okay," said Chelsi. "They're going to keep him at Dr. Cooper's for a few more days to watch him. And he'll have a cast on his back leg. We have to keep it clean and dry, but we can probably bring him home next week."

Annie nodded. "That's good." The lump in her throat

made it hard to talk.

"My parents told me what you did," said Chelsi. "You saved Spunk's life. You're about the best friend anybody could ever have. But it cost so much money . . . " Chelsi's voice cracked. "Are you still going to be able to buy Red?"

"No," Annie said softly.

"Oh. I'm sorry. He was just the coolest horse." Chelsi stopped, as if struggling for the right words. "Thank you for what you did. I know how much getting Red meant to you. I wish there was something I could do to pay you back. But I don't know if I ever can."

"It's okay," Annie said quietly.

After Chelsi left, Annie crept up to her room and curled up in a cocoon of covers. She heard her parents come in, talking in hushed tones, but she couldn't rouse herself to get up. She pulled an old teddy bear against her that she hadn't slept with in years. She was glad Spunky was alive, but she didn't quite know what to do with the big knot of disappointment swelling up inside her. *Maybe I was never meant to have a horse,* she thought. *Maybe not until I'm 40, or even 50 years old.* She wanted the weekend to be over, so she could go back to school and forget everything.

She went back to school on Monday, and on Tuesday, and on Wednesday. It was awful. Everyone knew she was supposed to be getting a horse named Red. So everyone stopped her in the hallway, on the playground, and in the lunchroom to ask about her new horse. She just hung her head and said, "I didn't get him." She didn't feel like going into the whole story.

Justin pestered her, though. In class, he whispered to her when Mrs. Finley had her back turned. "What happened, Annie?" he questioned. "I heard you saved

Chelsi's dog—that little mutt."

"He's not a mutt," said Annie fiercely.

"Well, I heard he would have died if it wasn't for you."
Annie's lip quivered.

"You used your horse money to pay for him? Wow,"
whispered Justin.

But the worst part was Chelsi. Usually at school they
did almost everything together. They passed notes in class.
They stood together in the lunch line. They played in the
same volleyball game. But now the air seemed strained
between them, like Chelsi was avoiding her. *You'd think
she'd be glad I saved her dog*, thought Annie. She didn't
know which made her feel worse—losing Red or not having
Chelsi to talk to.

Annie didn't know if she could take anymore days like
this. But on Wednesday afternoon, the phone rang and
Annie picked it up.

It was Chelsi. "Wanna come see the patient you saved?"

"Is he home?"

"Yes. He's here. He's supposed to stay in the house all
day, to keep his cast clean, except for potty breaks. He's got
to wear the cast for a few weeks. He's going to hate that. But
I think he's glad to be home. Why don't you come over?"

"Okay." Annie swallowed hard. "I've been missing the
little Spunk-dog." But that wasn't all she'd been missing.

Chelsi's mom, Mrs. Fidori, opened the door. "Hello,
Annie." She folded Annie against her in a deep hug. "I don't
know how we can ever repay you, honey."

Annie shrugged. "It's okay."

Spunky dragged himself into the front room, hobbling
tentatively. He smelled like the animal hospital, full of
antiseptic and medicines. His legs moved stiffly, as if he was

69

still getting used to carrying around the large cast attached to his left rear leg. But he had no problem moving his tail. It wagged so hard it seemed like it would knock the cast right off. There was no doubt that he recognized Annie as she knelt down on the floor to pet him.

"Hi, little guy," she said. "We were so worried about you." Spunky seemed awfully glad to see her, licking her face and hands, and rubbing his soft body against her. It was almost like he knew she needed some special comforting. Like he knew what part she had played in saving his life and at what cost.

Chelsi wandered in, her hands in her pockets. "Hi."

"He smells funny," said Annie.

"Yeah. Like a hospital, huh?"

"Were your parents mad at me?" asked Annie.

"My dad was a little upset." Chelsi looked into the kitchen to see if her mother was listening. "I think my dad feels bad that he can't pay you back. He was already mad that he lost his job, and then we couldn't afford to pay for Spunky. And when you did . . . it was kind of weird, you know?"

"Yeah." Annie sat in silence for a minute. "But are *you* mad?"

"No. Not at you. Never at you."

Spunky pushed his warm head under Annie's hand, then cuddled close against her. It made Annie feel as if she had made the right decision. So why did she still feel so empty inside?

Chapter Fourteen

School was almost out for the summer, and Spunky was on the road to recovery. Annie's days began to take on a sameness—one day just led into another. She got up in the morning, rode her bike to school, did her work diligently, and pedaled slowly home. She no longer raced home to get the newspaper. She never even looked at the classified ads. What was the use? She had no money now. And it would be a very long time before she could ever save enough money to buy another horse.

One afternoon, when she came home from school, her mom suggested that she go for a bike ride with Chelsi. "The sun is absolutely glorious today," said Mrs. Mitchell. "It will do you some good to get out in the fresh air." Annie reluctantly agreed.

Chelsi had to take Spunky outside for his walk first, and he limped carefully out into the side yard. Then she put him back inside the house where he lay on his special soft mat, and carefully shut the door. He still had a few weeks before his cast came off. "My dad fixed the tire on my bike," she said, "and he also fixed the gate where Spunky got out. He's putting electric wire around the whole bottom of the fence.

He said that once Spunky is better, he won't try to dig out after he bumps his nose into it just one time."

"Well, I guess it's for his own good," said Annie. Even though the thought of the electric wire fence made her squirm, it had to be all right if it kept Spunky safe.

As they rode their bikes down the hill towards the river, the warm wind rushed against Annie's face. It felt good. Soon it would be summer, and she would have a lot of time on her hands. She didn't want to think about a whole summer without a horse.

"My dad's getting a new job," said Chelsi. "It doesn't pay as much, but at least we won't have to move."

"I'm glad for that." At least Chelsi would be around for company.

They lazed along by the river, not finding much to talk about, and finally turning toward home. Chelsi took off ahead of Annie—her long, curly hair bopping up and down on her back. "Race you," she said.

"Okay, you're on," Annie yelled back. As she pedaled faster and faster, trying to catch up with her friend, she realized that Chelsi was headed down Walker Lane. Annie really didn't want to go that way. It would make her too sad to see the empty pasture. She had no choice, though, and she stood on the pedals of her bike, pumping hard to keep up with her friend.

As they got toward the end of the lane, they both slowed down to look. The sign that had said, "Pasture for Rent—$25 a month" was gone. Annie and Chelsi exchanged glances. The tall grass in the field looked trampled, and now there was a path around the inside perimeter of the fence line, where something had walked.

"Let's go," said Annie. She had worked so hard to get the

pasture ready for Red. She couldn't bear to see another horse in it.

But Chelsi had another idea. "Let's go ask Mr. Mendoza what's going on." She started off in that direction before Annie could stop her. Reluctantly, Annie rode slowly down the driveway, following her friend.

They knocked on the front door, but no answer. Just Pomeranians clawing at the window, making a racket at their presence. "I'm going home," said Annie, getting back on her bike.

"Maybe he's out back," said Chelsi.

"Hola, señoritas." Mr. Mendoza appeared from the back of his property. He held a can of chicken feed in his hand. "I'm glad you stopped by. Got something to show you."

Annie and Chelsi followed him towards the chicken pen. "Just let me grab a few eggs first," he said.

Annie scuffed the dirt with her toe. It made her sad to be reminded of the hours she had spent here—scrubbing the water tub, fixing the fence, getting the field ready for Red. She waited while Mr. Mendoza stooped under the low roof of the henhouse. Chickens scattered, making their way to the front of the pen. Annie heard a strange sound from the corner. Hesitant and tentative, it sounded like a rooster trying to crow, but not getting it quite right.

As Annie watched in amazement, she saw a young hen tilt back her head and try again. Crowing. The silly thing was trying to crow. It was definitely not a rooster. It was a hen!

"See, what did I tell you?" said Mr. Mendoza, his can full of eggs. "Didn't I tell you?"

"It's a hen," Annie gasped. "They do crow!" She put her hands over her mouth in surprise, not quite believing what

74

she was seeing. And she thought of her dad and his silly expressions. *When pigs fly. When hens crow. That's when I'll get a horse, he said.*

Mr. Mendoza set the can of eggs down on top of a box in the garage. "Now you girls just follow me," he said. "See what's out here."

Annie and Chelsi walked out past the chicken pen. Annie could see the back of the pasture from here. There was still a lot of tall grass, and there was a green hose running from Mr. Menodoza's faucet into the old bathtub that she had scrubbed. The tub was full of fresh, clean water.

Annie didn't want to look up. She didn't want to see what was in Red's pasture. But finally, she did. And she saw a pitiful, bony, old horse. Scroungy, with matted hair, it appeared to be cream-colored, almost white, underneath the manure that was caked on its coat. Annie could barely look at the pathetic thing.

The horse saw her, though. It nickered softly in greeting.

Chapter Fifteen

Annie's heart lurched when she heard the sound. She couldn't help it. It stirred up memories of Red and all the horses she had watched in fields since she was a tiny girl— every horse she had ever dreamed about all through her life.

But this was not Red. This horse was ugly and thin. A pitiful creature. "What happened to the poor thing?" she asked.

"Oh, my. It's had a hard time, I think. The last owner didn't feed his livestock, and someone finally called the sheriff. Hard to believe someone would treat an animal this way, isn't it?"

"But how did it get here?" Annie was curious now.

"Well, if they find serious enough abuse, Animal Control will confiscate the animals. That's what happened. They picked this old guy up, along with several others. It was one of the worst cases of animal neglect they've had in quite some time. Don't you listen to the news?"

Annie shook her head.

Mr. Mendoza whistled through his teeth. "Something like 22 horses, all being held in a pasture with no feed whatsoever. When Animal Control was finally called in, some of the horses were pretty far gone. Dr. Cooper had to put a few of them down."

Annie shuddered. "Dr. Cooper?"

"Well, with that many horses, they didn't have enough facilities for them all. They needed room. They are looking for foster homes for these poor horses."

"What's a foster home?" Chelsi asked.

"Someone who'll love these horses. Someone who will take real good care of them and nurse them back to health." Annie had been standing there quietly, taking all of this in. She strolled to the fence. The scrawny gelding reached his head over politely. She held her hand out flat, and he began licking it gently. It tickled.

"He's tasting the salt on your hand," said Mr. Mendoza. "He's going to need a salt block."

Annie reached up to feel the tangle of the horse's mane. She parted the white hair at the crest of his neck. She could see a swath of darker hair underneath.

"He's kind of ugly now. But when he finally sheds out, I think you'll find yourself with a palomino."

A palomino. Her favorite color. But what was Mr. Mendoza talking about? This wasn't her horse. This was a pathetic, ugly horse that belonged to someone who was mean to it. Who knew what would happen to the poor thing when the owner got it back? Annie looked up into the horse's soft eyes. The horse lowered its head, allowing Annie to scratch between his ears.

"Seems like kind of a gentle old thing, if you ask me," said Mr. Mendoza. "That's probably why Dr. Cooper had them bring it over here."

"What do you mean?" asked Annie.

"Well, these horses all need new owners, eventually.

77

They've been taken away permanently from the guy who abused them. He's being fined and will even do some jail time. Animal Control would like to find a kind person to spend some time with this horse—maybe end up owning him. Dr. Cooper seemed to think there might be someone around here who was interested. Would that be you?"

Annie suddenly understood what was happening. This was not Red. This was not the horse of her dreams. But this poor horse was right here in front of her. A horse to love, a horse that needed love. It was just like her dad had said— *when hens crow.*

The old horse lifted his head then, and she could almost imagine what he would look like when he put some weight back on and filled out. With a lot of brushing, she could get that matted dirt out of his coat, and she could comb the tangles from his mane and tail. She wanted to answer Mr. Mendoza. She wanted to tell him, yes, she would do it. She would make this horse's coat shine, make him strong and handsome again. I will take care of him, she tried to say. Just watch me. But Annie's words were all choked up inside of her.

The old horse pushed his scarred face over the fence. He nuzzled her gently, breathing in deeply, as if learning her scent. Annie wrapped her arms around his neck, burying her face against his knotted mane. Annie couldn't get her words out at all. Instead, she whispered. She whispered a promise directly into the ears of the old palomino gelding.